This Orchard book belongs to

....

....

spice

A

Sug

For
G, B
and P

ORCHARD BOOKS
338 Euston Road, London NW1 3BH
Orchard Books Australia
Level 17/207 Kent Street, Sydney,
NSW 2000

First published in 2010 by Orchard Books
First paperback publication in 2011
ISBN 978 1 40830 802 8

Text and illustrations
© Alison Murray 2010
The right of Alison Murray to be
identified as the author and illustrator
of this book has been asserted by her
in accordance with the Copyright,
Designs and Patents Act, 1988.

A CIP catalogue record for
this book is available
from the British Library.

10 9 8 7 6 5 4 3 2 1

Printed in China

Orchard Books is a division of
Hachette Children's Books,
an Hachette UK company.

www.hachette.co.uk

B

bake it

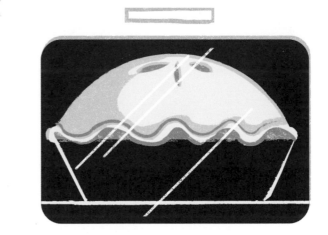

C
cool it

D
dish it out

eager for it

F

find a crumb of it

G

get a taste
for it

have to get a lick of it

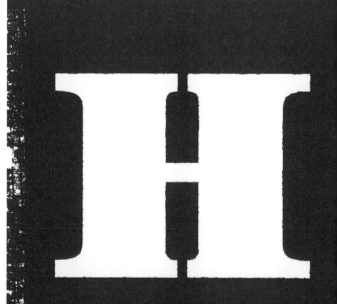

I

in trouble

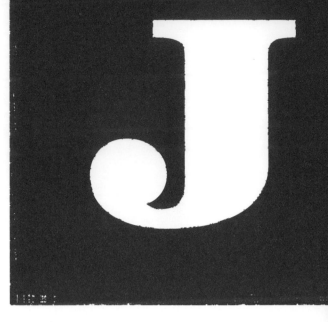

**jump up
for it**

K

**kept away
from it**

leave
without it

miserable

not giving up

O
ogle it

P
pine
for it

quietly
determined

R ready

S steady

T time to go for it

U

underneath it

V

very nearly . . .

W

whoops!

exit quickly

yum yum!

z z z z z z z

**go to sleep
and dream of it**

B

C